The Magic School Bus

CHAPTER BOOK

The Truth about BATS

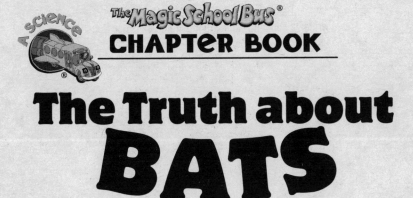

The Truth about BATS

SCHOLASTIC INC.
New York   Toronto   London   Auckland   Sydney
Mexico City   New Delhi   Hong Kong   Buenos Aires

Written by Eva Moore.

Illustrations by Ted Enik.

Based on *The Magic School Bus* books
written by Joanna Cole and illustrated by Bruce Degen.

No part of this publication may be reproduced in whole or in part, or stored in a retrieval system, or transmitted in any form or by any means, electronic, mechanical, photocopying, recording, or otherwise, without written permission of the publisher. For information regarding permission, write to Scholastic Inc., Attention: Permissions Department, 557 Broadway, New York, NY 10012.

ISBN 0-439-10798-9

60 59 58 57   13 14 15 16/0

Designed by Peter Koblish

Printed in the U.S.A.   40

Thanks to Jacqueline J. Belwood, Ph.D., Research Associate with the Ohio Biological Survey, and Dennis L. Krusac, Endangered Species Specialist, United States Department of Agriculture Forest Service, for their expert advice and consultation.

INTRODUCTION

My name is Ralphie. I am one of the kids in Ms. Frizzle's class.

Maybe you have heard of Ms. Frizzle. (Sometimes we just call her the Friz.) She is a terrific teacher — but strange. Her favorite subject is science, and she knows *everything*.

She takes us on lots of field trips in the Magic School Bus. Believe me, it's not called *magic* for nothing! We never know what's going to happen when we get on that bus.

Ms. Frizzle likes to surprise us, but we can usually tell when she is planning a special lesson — we just look at what she's wearing.

One day Ms. Frizzle picked this outfit out of her closet. That trip turned out to be some adventure! Let me tell you what happened.

CHAPTER 1

"Say cheese!" I aimed my camera at Tim and Dorothy Ann. We call her D.A. for short.

Click!

"What's up, Ralphie?" said Tim. "That's got to be the tenth time you've taken my picture this week."

"I just like to take pictures, that's all," I said. "My new camera is great. It was my favorite birthday present."

"Hurry up, you guys," D.A. said. "We'll be late for class."

It was almost time for summer vacation. Everyone was excited about the field trip that was coming up. We didn't know where we were

1

going, but with Ms. Frizzle for a teacher, we knew it would be far-out!

I caught up with Tim and D.A. at the door to our classroom. The rest of the class was already inside. Phoebe, Arnold, Wanda, and some of the other kids looked a little scared. I knew why the minute I saw the Friz. The dress she was wearing was covered with bats!

"Good morning, everyone!" Ms. Frizzle said. "Take your seats. I have wonderful news."

"Somehow, I don't think it's going to be so wonderful for me," Phoebe whispered to Wanda.

"As you know," the Friz went on, "we have one more field trip before school is out. And I have just the place. . . ." She went to the board and pulled down a map of the United States. She aimed her pointer at California. "Yosemite National Park! Home of majestic mountains, wonderful waterfalls, stupendous sequoia trees — and the rare and delightful spotted bat!"

"Everything sounds great except the bat part," Phoebe said. "I don't like them — they're ugly birds that suck your blood."

"Not so, Phoebe!" Ms. Frizzle said. "Check your bat facts."

"Ms. Frizzle is right," D.A. said. "First of all, bats are not birds. They are mammals, just like dogs and cats — and us. They are the only mammals that can fly. That's pretty neat!"

"Yes," Keesha said. "And they don't suck people's blood. That's just a myth."

"Vampire bats *do* eat blood, but from cattle and horses, not people," D.A. added. "They don't really suck the blood. They make a slit and lap up a few drops."

"We won't be running into vampire bats in California anyhow," Tim told Phoebe. "They live mostly in Central and South America, not in the United States. Vampire bats are just one kind of bat."

"Aha!" Ms. Frizzle said. "You're *bat*ting a thousand there, Tim."

Fur and Feathers
by Dorothy Ann

Mammals are animals that have fur. They give birth to live young and nurse their offspring with milk.

Birds are animals that have feathers. They lay eggs in nests and keep them warm until the young birds hatch.

Ms. Frizzle put a disk in the computer and punched some keys. A bat with huge pink ears and black-and-white spotted fur appeared on the monitor.

"There it is! The spotted bat. These bats live in western North America. Yosemite is one of the few places in California where they have been seen."

"Get a load of those pink ears," Carlos said. "These guys look like the bunnies of the bat world."

"I thought all bats were black," Wanda said.

"Some are black, some are brown, or gray, or red, or silver, or — spotted!" said the Friz.

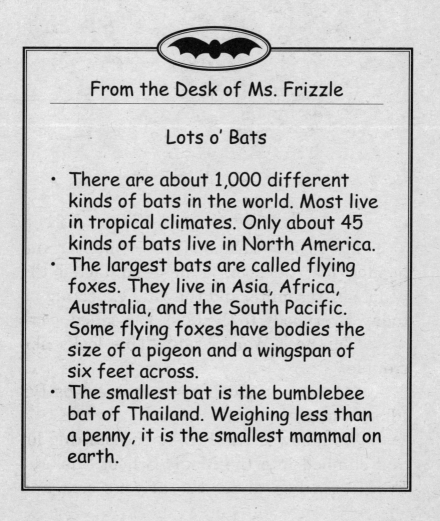

From the Desk of Ms. Frizzle

Lots o' Bats

- There are about 1,000 different kinds of bats in the world. Most live in tropical climates. Only about 45 kinds of bats live in North America.
- The largest bats are called flying foxes. They live in Asia, Africa, Australia, and the South Pacific. Some flying foxes have bodies the size of a pigeon and a wingspan of six feet across.
- The smallest bat is the bumblebee bat of Thailand. Weighing less than a penny, it is the smallest mammal on earth.

"And different kinds of bats live in different locations," Ms. Frizzle added.

Ms. Frizzle turned off the computer and headed for the door. "I have contacted the people in Yosemite, and they are expecting us today. Everybody, to the bus!" she called.

"Oh, gee," Wanda said. "This looks like trouble."

"At my old school, we never went batty," Phoebe said.

We followed the Friz to the parking lot and climbed into the Magic School Bus. Ms. Frizzle reached under the driver's seat and pulled out a cap like the ones that airline pilots wear. She put it on and pushed some buttons on the dashboard.

The next thing we knew the bus was tearing along like a jet plane. Wait! It really *was* a jet plane. I felt the force of the bus-jet's speed push me against the back of my seat. In a moment, we were airborne.

California, here we come!

✦CHAPTER 2✦

Very soon, the bus-jet was above the clouds. Ms. Frizzle was wearing a jumpsuit with pictures of a pink-eared bat — the famous spotted bat of Yosemite. Most of us were enjoying the ride. Phoebe was biting her fingernails and looking nervous.

We'd studied bats before, but some of us still secretly believed that they were scary. Me? I think they're cool — from a distance. I like the way they rest hanging upside down with their wings folded around them. For bats, upside down is right side up!

Phoebe had some funny ideas about bats. "Who can tell what a bat will do?" she said. "I heard a story about a woman who was out walking in broad daylight — and a stupid blind bat flew right into her hair!"

Keesha laughed. "That's just a story. Bats aren't blind. They can see fine, but for most kinds of bats, vision isn't as important as their other senses."

"And there's another big reason why that story must be made-up," Arnold said. "Tell her, Ms. Frizzle."

"Bats don't accidentally fly into things, Phoebe," the Friz said. "They have built-in sonar that helps them get around — even in the dark."

"I know about sonar," Wanda said. "Bats make clicking sounds as they fly through the air. The clicks are ultrasonic, meaning they are too high-pitched for humans to hear. The clicks bounce off every object around, no matter how small, and echo back to the bat. That's how they are able to go hunting for food at night."

"You got it, Wanda!" Ms. Frizzle said.

"There are a lot of myths about bats,"

Ms. Frizzle told us. "People didn't know much about them in the old days. Bats are so mysterious that people still believe a lot of the myths, but they're not true."

What is an echo?
                    by Wanda

An echo is a reflection of sound. Location is the act of locating, or finding, where something is. So, echolocation is the act of finding something by the echoes it makes.

"And don't forget that most bats are night animals," Tim said. "They are just going to sleep when we get up. There's no way a little bat would be out flying around in broad daylight."

"Oh, yeah," Phoebe said. "If that's true, how are we going to see this famous spotted bat?"

From the Desk of Ms. Frizzle

Bats, Whales, and Dolphins: How Are They Alike?

The way that bats use ultrasonic sounds to locate objects around them is called echolocation.

Whales and dolphins are two other kinds of mammals that use echolocation. Their sound waves go through the water, while the bats' sound waves go through the air.

"Do we get to stay up late?" Keesha asked.

"We sure do, Keesha!" Ms. Frizzle announced. "We're going to camp out so we will be right at the scene."

"Oh, good. I love to go camping!" Phoebe smiled for once. At last there was something about this trip she was looking forward to.

Suddenly the bus-jet started beeping. "It's the bat-o-meter," Ms. Frizzle explained. "It says we're flying over a large colony of cave-dwelling bats. This is something we have to see."

Ms. Frizzle pushed a few buttons on the control panel. Overhead, we heard a *thit thit thit thit* sound, like a helicopter's blades. The Friz had turned our jet into a helicopter!

She set the bus-copter down on a flat rock.

"Here are your bat explorer kits." Ms. Frizzle gave everyone a pack with a hard hat, a flashlight, and a pair of boots. "Hurry up, now," she called. "It's our turn at bat!"

From the Desk of Ms. Frizzle

For Bats, Night Is Right!

Why nighttime is a good time for a bat to be out and about:

1. Its thin wings would get hot in the sun and cause the bat to lose too much water.

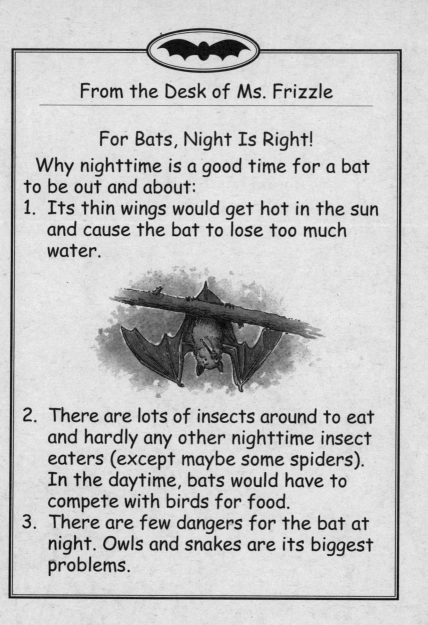

2. There are lots of insects around to eat and hardly any other nighttime insect eaters (except maybe some spiders). In the daytime, bats would have to compete with birds for food.
3. There are few dangers for the bat at night. Owls and snakes are its biggest problems.

CHAPTER 3

Halfway up a mountain ridge we came upon a large, dark hole.

"Cool!" said Tim. "Let's see what's inside."

"I'll wait out here," Phoebe announced. "There's no way I'm going in there."

"I'm with you," Arnold and Wanda said at the same time.

"Come on, you guys," said Keesha. "We have our flashlights, and we'll be together. There's nothing to be afraid of."

"Except man-eating bats!" Phoebe said.

"Yeah," Arnold told Keesha. "Why don't you go in and then tell us about it? If you come back alive."

Ms. Frizzle put on a hard hat with a headlamp on it. "Follow me and stay quiet," she said.

D.A. took Phoebe's hand and pulled her into the tunnel behind Ms. Frizzle. The rest of us followed.

Where Do Bats Hang Out?
by Arnold

Bats like to hang out in dark, quiet places. Some choose caves. Others find good roosting places in trees, barns, or attics of houses.

It sure was spooky. Our flashlights made little circles of light on the walls of the tunnel, but we were surrounded by darkness. The air was damp and much cooler. I felt goose bumps popping out all over my arms and legs.

The tunnel opened up and we found ourselves deep in the cave.

"Yuck!" Carlos said. "What's this stuff we're stepping in?"

"That's bat guano," D.A. said. "Good thing we have these boots."

"You can say that again!" Carlos said.

What Is Bat Guano?

by Carlos

Bat guano is another name for bat poop! Bat guano can be used to make fertilizer for plants. Bat guano is rich in nitrogen, a chemical that helps plants grow.

"Ah, this looks like the bat sleeping quarters," Ms. Frizzle said. She looked up and the headlight on her hard hat lit the ceiling.

It was covered with bats — hundreds of them hanging upside down.

"Uh-oh!" Ms. Frizzle said. "Those are gray bats up there — an endangered species. And some of them are only half-grown pups.

This must be a nursery colony. We have to get out of here."

We didn't know why the Friz was so upset, but everyone turned around and followed her out of the nursery colony. Then I got an idea. It would take just a second to snap a picture. I put my flashlight on the floor and aimed my camera at the ceiling.

Click! The light flashed as I pushed the shutter button.

Some of the bats started flapping their wings. The flash must have woken them up! I turned around and ran.

But I had left my flashlight in the cave. I couldn't see a thing. I took a few steps and bumped right into a wall. I didn't know which way to turn, so I did the only thing I could think of.

"Help! Help!" I yelled.

"Help! Help!" the cave echoed back.

No one came. I was alone in a cave full of bats.

CHAPTER 4

I was lost in the dark tunnel and getting colder by the minute. I kept yelling but my voice was giving out. Where was Ms. Frizzle?

At last I thought I saw a glimmer in the dark. The light grew larger and larger. "Ms. Frizzle!" I yelled.

"Ralphie!" she said. "What are you doing?"

"I was taking a picture of the bats," I explained. "But my flash woke them up and I was afraid they would attack me. I left my flashlight behind."

"*You* probably scared *them*," Ms. Frizzle said. "It's time we were out of here. Follow me."

Everyone was waiting for us outside the cave. Was I glad to see the gang!

"Ralphie made a mistake," Ms. Frizzle said. "You see, gray bats have pups just once a year. Ralphie could have upset the mothers or caused these newborn pups to fall, and that would have been real trouble for this colony. As it is, gray bats are one of the most endangered mammals in this country."

"You mean they're in danger of becoming extinct?" Tim asked. "How come?"

"Gray bats need caves to live in, Tim," Ms. Frizzle said. "But lots of caves are being destroyed these days. People want to use the land for other things, such as houses."

"Can't the bats just move to other caves, like this one?" Wanda asked.

"Sooner or later, they'll run out of caves," Ms. Frizzle explained. "That's why scientists are trying to protect the caves now. In fact, most gray-bat homes have a gate across the entrance and a sign warning people to keep out. It's against the law to go inside." She paused.

How Bats Help

by Tim

   Bats are important to us because
they eat tons of insects that are
harmful to animals, crops, and people.
   Some even pollinate flowers as they
feed, helping new plants to grow.

"Hmm," she said, "I'm surprised this cave is still open. I'll have to report it to the Fish and Wildlife Service."

Now I felt bad. I didn't mean to harm the bats.

"I just wanted to get a couple of good pictures for my album," I told Ms. Frizzle.

"A bunch of sleeping gray bats isn't a very exciting picture," Arnold said. "You need to get a shot of a fierce flying bat with its mouth open so you can see its sharp teeth. *That* would be something else!"

"It's perfectly natural for bats to fly with their mouths open," Ms. Frizzle pointed out. "They're not being fierce at all. They're just using echolocation to 'see' you. Most bats send out their sonar signals through their mouths."

"I didn't know that," Phoebe said. "But I've seen photos of bats in books, and lots of them are snarling."

"You'd snarl, too, if someone trapped you and held you down to take your picture. The bat is just scared and trying to defend itself," Ms. Frizzle said.

"Yeah," D.A. added. "Like my kitten, Teddy, when another cat comes around. He folds his ears back and shows his teeth and spits. He looks so fierce — but he doesn't usually look that way."

From the Desk of Ms. Frizzle

Sound Signals

Some kinds of bats send out sonar signals through their noses instead of their mouths.

Most flying foxes don't use sonar to hunt for food. They use their eyes and noses.

"Do you know another way that bats are like cats?" Tim asked.

"They rhyme?" Wanda guessed.

"Very funny. Try again," said Tim.

"Well, they both have fur," said Wanda.

"Yes," said Tim, "but that's not all. Bats clean themselves — just like cats — by licking their fur. They are very clean animals."

Ms. Frizzle checked her watch. "We're running late," she said. "Back to the copter. We should be in California by now."

"Wait!" I said. "Let me take some shots of us at the cave."

Everyone lined up in front of the cave.

"Let's pretend we're flying gray bats!" Keesha said. The kids crouched with their arms spread and opened their mouths.

Click! Another great shot for my album. Then Tim took a picture of me.

"Come on, class!" Ms. Frizzle called from the cockpit. We climbed into the bus-copter and took off in a cloud of whirling dust.

Before we knew it, the bus-copter turned into a bus-jet and we were off to California.

CHAPTER 5

The bus-jet made a steep turn and headed downward. Below we could see snow-capped mountains above green valleys. Rivers that looked like shiny ribbons snaked their way through the valley.

This was Yosemite National Park!

"Prepare to land," called the Friz. She pushed the button on the control panel that turned the jet into a copter.

Ms. Frizzle set the bus-copter down in the valley near a parking area. We piled out and stood staring at the sight. All around us were humongous mountains. One looked as if a chunk had been sliced off the top. We could see three waterfalls tumbling down the sides of tall stone cliffs.

"That big one must be Yosemite Falls," D.A. said. "It's the largest waterfall in the country."

Now I was really glad I had my camera. I started snapping like crazy.

"Better save some film for later, Ralphie," D.A. said. "There are a lot of other fabulous sights here."

A man wearing a green uniform and a hat with a wide brim came up to us.

"Welcome to Yosemite, Ms. Frizzle," he said. "I got your e-mail. Everything is ready for tonight."

"Class, this is Ranger Mike," Ms. Frizzle said. "He's going to be our guide."

Ranger Mike smiled. "Hello, everybody. I'm mighty glad to know you."

"Thank you for coming to meet us, Ranger," said Ms. Frizzle. "We are looking forward to our stay. Now, if you would be so kind — show me the way to the spotted bat!"

She turned and walked to the place

where the bus-copter had landed. And there was our school bus! It was good to see it back in its normal form.

Phoebe groaned. "Just when I was starting to have fun," she said. "I almost forgot why we came."

"Well, I know that Ms. Frizzle has her heart set on seeing the spotted bat," Ranger Mike said to us, "but I can't promise we'll find one. There's no way of telling what kind of bats we will catch tonight when we go mist-netting."

"What's mist-netting?" Wanda asked.

"You'll see," said Ranger Mike as he got into his Jeep. "Okay, Ms. Frizzle!" he called. "After me."

The bus followed the Jeep along a road that twisted and turned as it climbed higher into the mountains. Soon we turned off the main highway and onto a road that went through the woods. Pine trees towered above us.

We stopped at a clearing near a river that looked as smooth as glass.

"Home sweet home!" Ms. Frizzle sang out. "What a great campsite!"

We stepped off the bus and looked around.

"Where are the cabins?" Arnold asked. "Where are the beds? There's nothing here but grass and trees."

Ms. Frizzle knew that Arnold did not always like to rough it. Oops, I think I got that wrong. Arnold *never* liked to rough it.

"Never fear, the bus is here!" she said. She pressed a lever at the front of the bus.

Instantly, the sides folded out and formed themselves into a log-cabin shape.

We ran inside.

"It's so neat!" Wanda said when she saw the huge sofa in front of a round woodstove. At the other end of the bus-cabin were bunk beds covered with red woolly blankets.

"It's even got a bathroom!" Arnold exclaimed.

This was his kind of camping — all the comforts of home.

CHAPTER 6

Ranger Mike had pitched his tent next to the bus-cabin.

"We'd better start setting up the nets now, Ms. Frizzle," he said. He disappeared into the tent for a few minutes. When he came out, he had on long black boots that came up to his hips.

Ms. Frizzle put on long boots, too. But hers had red bat shapes on them.

"We need these hip waders," Ranger Mike explained, "because we'll be going into the river. That water is mighty cold this time of year."

Ranger Mike unfolded a square of fine, black netting. It looked like a huge hair net.

"We call this a 'mist net' because it's as filmy as mist," the ranger said.

Ms. Frizzle took some tall poles and waded across the river. In about half an hour, she and Ranger Mike had stretched two mist nets across the river. One net was higher than the other. They were nearly invisible.

"The nets are right above places where bats come to hunt insects," Ranger Mike explained.

"You mean the bats are going to fly right into the nets and get trapped?" Tim asked.

"*Some* bats will get caught because their sonar won't pick up the netting fast enough," Ranger Mike said. "The net doesn't hurt them, and this is one way scientists learn about where different kinds of bats live. The bats are identified and counted — and then they are let go."

"Why are there two nets?" Wanda asked.

"Some kinds of bats fly low and some fly

high," Ranger Mike told her. "The spotted bat, for example, flies high, so we need the higher net if we hope to catch one. In the lower net we might get some Yummies."

"Yummies?" we all asked at once.

"We're not going to eat them, are we?" Arnold asked. He looked a little sick.

"Don't worry, kids. That's just a nickname for the Yuma bat," said the ranger. "It is one of the most common bats around here. But we might catch other kinds, too. Yosemite has fifteen different types of bats."

"That's fifteen too many for me," Phoebe said. "May I be excused?"

D.A. went to stand beside her. "Don't worry, Phoebe," she said. "The bats won't bother us."

Just then we heard the clanging of a bell. "Chow time!" called Ms. Frizzle. She had changed into another bat outfit and had a campfire going on the bank of the river.

"We're having a cookout!" Carlos said.

"Hot dogs, hamburgers, baked beans, and potato chips!" Arnold said. "All right!"

Everybody dug in and enjoyed the cook-out — even Phoebe. As the sun went down, we sat around the fire roasting marshmallows.

"Ouch!" I cried and slapped my neck. "Mosquitoes!"

"They're biting me, too," Wanda said. "I hate mosquitoes."

Ranger Mike looked out over the river. It was nearly dark.

"The insects are out," Ranger Mike said. "It's time for the bats to wake up."

"*Now* may I be excused?" Phoebe asked.

"But the fun is just beginning," Ms. Frizzle told her. "Here are your night peepers. Put them on, and you will be able to see in the dark."

It was terrific! With the special glasses I could see almost as if it were daytime.

"I think we just got one in the net!" Ranger Mike called. He waded into the river and came back with something cupped in his hands.

"It's a Yum-yum," he said. "A young Yuma."

"That's a bat?" Phoebe said. "It looks more like a brown cotton ball."

"It's a bat, all right." Ranger Mike gently pulled on the wings so that we could see the shape.

"The bat's wings are something like our hands, with a thumb and fingers," the ranger pointed out. "Sometimes bats use their wings to catch insects. The bat traps the insect against its body, then eats it up."

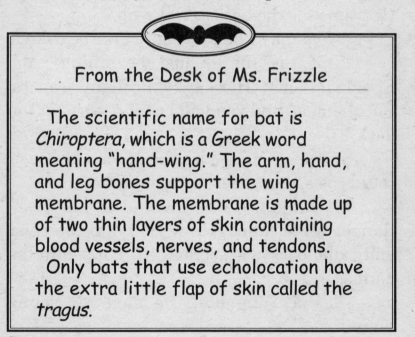

From the Desk of Ms. Frizzle

The scientific name for bat is *Chiroptera*, which is a Greek word meaning "hand-wing." The arm, hand, and leg bones support the wing membrane. The membrane is made up of two thin layers of skin containing blood vessels, nerves, and tendons.

Only bats that use echolocation have the extra little flap of skin called the *tragus*.

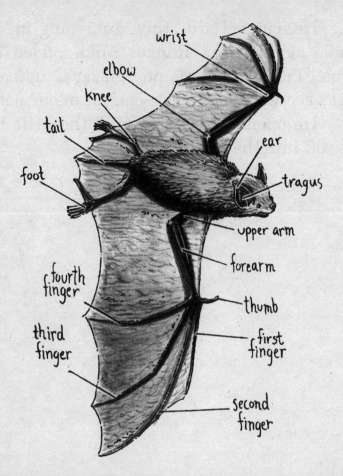

wrist

elbow

knee

tail

foot

ear

tragus

upper arm

forearm

fourth finger

thumb

third finger

first finger

second finger

"I didn't know that a bat has fingers and thumbs," Phoebe said.

"Bats are amazing creatures," Ranger Mike said. "The more you know about them, the more you like them."

He cupped the tiny Yum-yum in his hands again. Then Ranger Mike raised his arms. "I'm letting this one go now," he said. "Let's see what else we've caught in our nets."

He opened his hands and the little bat flew off into the night.

CHAPTER 7

The class stood on the bank of the river watching bats zipping in from all directions.

"These night peepers are the greatest," Keesha said. "Look how fast those bats zero in on the insects."

"That's their sonar at work!" Ms. Frizzle said.

Most of the bats darted over or around the mist nets, but every now and then one got caught.

"Here's a big brown," Ranger Mike called as he untangled a struggling bat.

"It doesn't look very big to me," Carlos

said when Ranger Mike showed us the brown furry creature clinging to his glove.

"It's a medium-sized bat, really," the ranger told us. "Bigger than its cousin, the little brown bat. With its wings folded up like this, it looks small. But in the air, the wings spread out to more than a foot across."

"There are big brown bats in my neighborhood," D.A. said. "I've never seen one, but the people down the street had one in their attic one summer."

"That's not surprising, D.A.," Ranger Mike said. "Brown bats, big and little, get around. In the U.S. they live in all forty-eight of the continental states."

No sooner had we let the big brown bat go than we had more action at the nets.

"Oh dear, oh dear! Look what's coming in now!" Keesha cried.

We turned around to see a flier with enormous wings, maybe two feet across, swooping above the river. In the next instant it seemed to stop in midair. It had flown right into the taller mist net.

How to Find a Bug
by Keesha

  The bat sends out a series of ultrasonic clicks as it flies through the air. As the bat comes closer to the insect, the clicks get faster. The ultrasonic waves bounce off the insect and back to the bat's ears.

"Is it a bird?" Phoebe asked.

"No need to worry about that, Phoebe," said Ms. Frizzle. "The birds are already asleep. Unless I miss my guess, our visitor is wearing fur, not feathers."

"You're right, Ms. Frizzle," Ranger Mike said. "This is a bat — and then some! Come and meet the western mastiff, the largest bat in the U.S.A."

Phoebe started to back away, but D.A. grabbed her hand. "Come on, Phoebe. You don't want to miss this."

Ranger Mike held the mastiff gently but firmly. Its body was almost as long as his hand.

"It has the face of a dog!" Carlos said. "Weird."

"Does it bite?" Phoebe asked.

"Only in self-defense," Ranger Mike explained. "But it's best not to mess around with any bats. Some have strong jaws and could give you a bad bite."

"Then you could die!" cried Phoebe.

"Bats carry a bad disease called rabies. That's what I've heard."

"Yes, a few bats do have rabies," said D.A. "But most bats are healthy. Skunks and foxes are more likely to have rabies than bats."

"True," Ranger Mike said. "But even though bats probably will not harm you, you should never try to pick up a bat or any other wild animal. Leave that to experts like me."

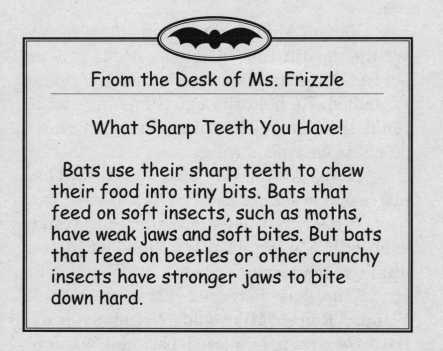

From the Desk of Ms. Frizzle

What Sharp Teeth You Have!

Bats use their sharp teeth to chew their food into tiny bits. Bats that feed on soft insects, such as moths, have weak jaws and soft bites. But bats that feed on beetles or other crunchy insects have stronger jaws to bite down hard.

A Word from Dorothy Ann

Some animals that have rabies act wild and even foam at the mouth. But a sick bat seems quiet and tame. Don't be fooled. Any bat that will let you get close to it is probably sick.

Ranger Mike had to climb onto a rock to set the mastiff free. "This one needs at least six feet of free fall to get airborne," the ranger explained. He held the mastiff as high as he could, then let go. The bat dipped, then soared off on its enormous wings.

It was getting very late, and we still had not seen one spot of Ms. Frizzle's spotted bat.

"I hope that bat shows up soon," Wanda said with a yawn. "I don't think I can stay awake much longer."

"The bat may not show up at all, Wanda," Ranger Mike said. "Not many people have ever seen a spotted bat, and we don't know much about its habits. We think these bats might live in the cliffs near our rivers and lakes. One was caught here in Yosemite a few years ago."

"How big is it?" Wanda wanted to know.

"About the size of the big brown," Ranger Mike said. "It eats mostly moths, and has a voice like no other bat. People are more likely to hear it than to see it."

"Hear it?" Keesha asked. "I thought we couldn't hear bats."

"We can't hear bat calls that are ultrasonic," Ranger Mike said. "But some bats, such as the spotted bat, make echolocation sounds that are not quite so high-pitched. People can hear them very well."

"Does the call of the spotted bat sound anything like *that*?" Ms. Frizzle asked. We all stood still and listened, trying to hear what Ms. Frizzle had heard. First, there was nothing. Then a harsh, high-pitched *tic tic tic tic* filled the air.

"That's it!" Ranger Mike whispered. "That's the spotted bat!"

"Where? Where?" We all turned toward the sound and stared as hard as we could through our night peepers.

Then Ms. Frizzle walked to the edge of the river and pulled a little net bag from the pocket of her bat outfit. She opened it — and out flew a cloud of silvery moths. They seemed to blink like fireflies in the darkness.

In the next instant, the dark shape of a bat came zooming in. It flew over our heads and we could see the white belly of the spotted bat! It caught several moths and was swooping down for another when it flew right into our mist net.

CHAPTER 8

"Amazing!" Ranger Mike said. He waded into the cold water and carefully untangled the prize.

"Well, Ms. Frizzle," he said as he came back onshore with the bat, "we're mighty lucky tonight."

He held up the bat with one hand, and we crowded around. Even Phoebe was eager to get a look at this unusual catch.

"Where are the spots?" D.A. asked.

Ranger Mike turned the bat so we could see its furry back. Three white spots showed brightly on its black fur.

"Check out those bunny ears," Carlos said. "Just like in the picture Ms. Frizzle showed us."

Ranger Mike stroked the long fur with his finger. "I've read that some spotted bats don't like to be held. But this one doesn't seem to mind," he said.

The next thing I knew, I was reaching out. I touched the bat's back with my finger! It really *was* furry.

"Ralphie!" Wanda almost screamed. "You touched a bat."

"Hey, he's not bad," I said. I started petting the bat with *two* fingers. "He seems to like me. I'm going to call him Bugs, because of his big ears."

"Let me try," Carlos said. "I like those pink ears."

"Just this once," said Ranger Mike. "We couldn't do this with every wild animal, but Bugs seems to be taking it in stride."

One by one, all the kids stepped up to pet Bugs.

Last came D.A. and Phoebe.

"You first," Phoebe said. D.A. stroked the bat. "See, he's a good bat. Go ahead and touch him, Phoebe. You'll be surprised."

"Phoebe will never do it," Tim blurted out. "She has bat-o-phobia."

"I do not," said Phoebe. "I don't even know what that is."

"It means you're afraid of bats," Carlos told her.

"Oh, yeah?" Phoebe took a deep breath and lifted her hand.

"Wait!" I cried. "I have to get a picture of this!" I ran into the bus-cabin and got my camera.

Phoebe touched Bugs and gave a little squeal. Then she grinned. I pushed the shutter button. *Click!* Another great shot for my album.

"I really like Bugs," Phoebe said. "Could we take him back to school with us, Ms. Frizzle? He could be our class pet. It would be fun to have a lizard *and* a bat."

"I wish we could, Phoebe," Ms. Frizzle said. "But as my cousin Bea Free says, 'A wild animal's home is a place where it can roam.' Bugs needs wide-open spaces to survive." She gave the bat an extra-special pat.

"Not only that, kids," Ranger Mike said. "This bat is too precious to nature for us to even think about taking him away from his home. Spotted bats are on the government's list of "rare" animals that need special protection. I never thought I would ever see one this close."

"Yes, I guess it would be a shame to take Bugs away from this beautiful place," Phoebe said.

"I'm sure he will be glad to get back to his cliff," Ranger Mike said.

Ranger Mike lifted Bugs up as high as he could. The bat took off, ears pointing forward as it took to the air.

"Good-bye, Bugs," we called. We all waved until we could not see him anymore.

CHAPTER 9

After Bugs had disappeared from view, Ms. Frizzle and Ranger Mike started to take down the mist nets. We headed for the bunk beds in the bus-cabin and wrapped ourselves in the red woolly blankets.

The next thing I knew, the sun was coming in the bus-cabin windows.

"Rise and shine, sleepyheads," Ms. Frizzle called. "It's almost afternoon. You must be starving."

Ms. Frizzle had fixed a big lunch for us — hot dogs, hamburgers, baked beans, and potato chips. Yum. The food was as good today as it had been the night before.

"Time for some fun in the sun," Ms. Frizzle said. "Ranger Mike has a surprise for you."

There on the river was a bright orange rubber boat with a motor. "Everybody grab a life preserver," called Ranger Mike, "and come onboard!"

"Cool!" D.A. said.

We climbed into the boat and Ranger Mike pulled the cord to start the motor. Wheee! We flew along the river like the wind.

We stopped at the base of a waterfall and climbed the steps up the cliff to the top. Ranger Mike posed for a picture with the class. *Click!* Another great shot for my album.

"This turned out to be fun after all," Arnold said.

"The best," Phoebe agreed.

It was hard to believe that the day was almost over.

Ranger Mike took us back upriver to the bus-cabin. "Have a good trip home," he said. "I'm mighty glad you came. So long, and have a good summer." He got into his Jeep and drove off down the road.

"To the bus!" Ms. Frizzle called. The bus-cabin seemed to whirl around in a blur. When it stopped, it had changed into the copter again.

Ms. Frizzle pushed the control buttons and we lifted off. Soon the copter turned into a jet and we were above the snowy peaks of Yosemite, heading east.

We hadn't been airborne for long when the bat-o-meter started beeping like mad.

"Get ready!" the Friz called from the cockpit. "We're making one more stop."

"Now what?" Arnold said.

"I have a funny feeling we're about to meet some more bats," I said.

I was right.

Not much later we landed in a parking lot in a large city. The Friz came out of the cockpit wearing a cowboy hat and boots.

"Welcome to Texas, the battiest state in

the country." Ms. Frizzle passed out cowboy hats for us all. "No other state is home to so many different kinds of bats — thirty-two at last count. We're in the capital city of Austin, a very special place for bats. You'll see what I mean."

We followed Ms. Frizzle to a bridge in the middle of the busy city. The sun was setting, and a lot of people were standing along the railings. They looked as if they were waiting for something to happen.

As the sun went down, the clouds turned deep purple. Some bats flew out from underneath the bridge — then dozens more. A few circled above us, right over our heads. Soon the sky was filled with hundreds of flying bats — maybe even thousands!

"These are Mexican free-tailed bats, class," Ms. Frizzle told us. "Each summer more than a million of them return to this bridge from Mexico to have their young. The people of Austin are always glad to see them again. And no wonder — the bats eat from

15,000 to 30,000 pounds of insects in a single night!"

"I guess bats really are our friends," Phoebe said. "And that's no myth."

I checked my camera. There was only one shot left on the roll. I aimed at the stream of soaring wings beneath the purple clouds and *click!*

Another great picture for my album.

Let's Help Bats
                              by Phoebe

Every year thousands of bats are destroyed by pesticides, poisons, or senseless killing. Fewer bats mean more insects; more insects mean more disease and more damage to crops that provide the food we eat. We should all do our part to protect the bats that dive and dart in the night sky.

Soon we were back in the bus-jet on our way home.

"I can't wait to see all the pictures you took, Ralphie," Wanda said.

"Me either," I said. "I'll bring them to school when I get them developed."

A few days later, I walked into Ms. Frizzle's room with my photo album. Everyone gathered around.

"Look at us at the gray-bat cave!" Tim said. "I hope that they've put a gate on it by now."

"I like this one of Ranger Mike setting up the mist net," Wanda said. "He was a nice guy."

It was easy to see what Phoebe's favorite picture was.

"Oh, here I am with Bugs," she said. "I'll never forget that little spotted bat."

I knew that was true for all of us.

Guess the ANSWERS

Ms. Frizzle's class learned a lot about bats on their field trip to Yosemite. But they still had some questions when they got back to the classroom.

Here are their questions — and the answers.

1. Arnold asks:
How long does a bat usually live?

Bats have a longer life span than other mammals their size. Small rodents, like mice, for example, live only one or two years. But bats that survive their first winter may live many, many years. The average is about fifteen. Some live to be in their twenties, and some even get to be thirty years old!

2. D.A. asks:
Do all bats live in colonies?

No. Many kinds of bats live and feed together in groups of a few to a few thousand. But some bats, such as the red bat and the hoary bat, go out on their own. Individuals hunt and sleep by themselves in trees. These bats get together at mating time; then mothers stay together when raising pups. Also, some that spend the summer in northern areas may go south together in the winter.

3. *Phoebe asks:*
How does a mother bat in a large colony tell which pup is hers?

A newborn pup clings to its mother's body until it is half-grown. Then it hangs beside her until it is ready to fly off on its own. If the two get separated, the baby sends out a special SOS call. It keeps calling until its mother comes. She can tell by the pup's voice and smell that the baby is hers.

4. *Carlos asks:*
How fast can a bat fly?

The Mexican free-tailed bat flies 35 miles an hour at top speed, but the big brown bat is the record holder. It zips along at 40 miles an hour.

Fast-flying bats can cover a lot of ground. Some free-tailed bats were seen to travel a distance of 85 miles in no more than two nights. That's over 40 miles a night!

5. *Wanda asks:*

Humans can't hear a bat's echolocation calls, but other bats can. How loud do the calls sound to them?

The echolocation sounds of most bats are really earsplitting to other bats — about as loud as a smoke detector going off! Luckily for the bat, it has special muscles that close its ears whenever it sends out signals. If it didn't have these muscles, the bat would make itself deaf.

6. *Keesha asks:*
How can I get insect-eating bats to come and live in my backyard?

Since the 1980s, thousands of Americans have put up special wooden bat houses to attract bats to parks, forests, and backyards.

A bat house that is just two feet tall and wide and five to six inches deep can attract nursery colonies of as many as two hundred to three hundred bats!

Bat Box

Side view

Landing Platform

You can buy or make a bat house yourself. For information contact Bat Conservation International, P.O. Box 162603, Austin, TX 20716.
Internet address: http//www.batcon.org.

Join my class on all of our Magic School Bus adventures!

The Truth about Bats
The Search for the Missing Bones
The Wild Whale Watch
Space Explorers
Twister Trouble
The Giant Germ
The Great Shark Escape
Penguin Puzzle
Dinosaur Detectives
Expedition Down Under
Insect Invaders
Amazing Magnetism
Polar Bear Patrol
Electric Storm
Voyage to the Volcano
Butterfly Battle
Food Chain Frenzy

The Magic School Bus™

Climb on board & catch the fun with these ALL NEW DVDs of the Magic School Bus television series!

Available at a retailer near you and online at:
scholasticstore.com and **warnervideo.com**

The Magic School Bus
Bugs, Bugs, Bugs!

Scholastic's The Magic School Bus
Creepy, Crawly Fun!

Scholastic's The Magic School Bus
Space Adventures

The Magic School Bus®
Super Sports Fun

NEW DVDs
coming Fall 2005
from the Magic School Bus
television series.

*The Magic School Bus
Catches a Wave*
•
*The Magic School Bus
Human Body*

■SCHOLASTIC